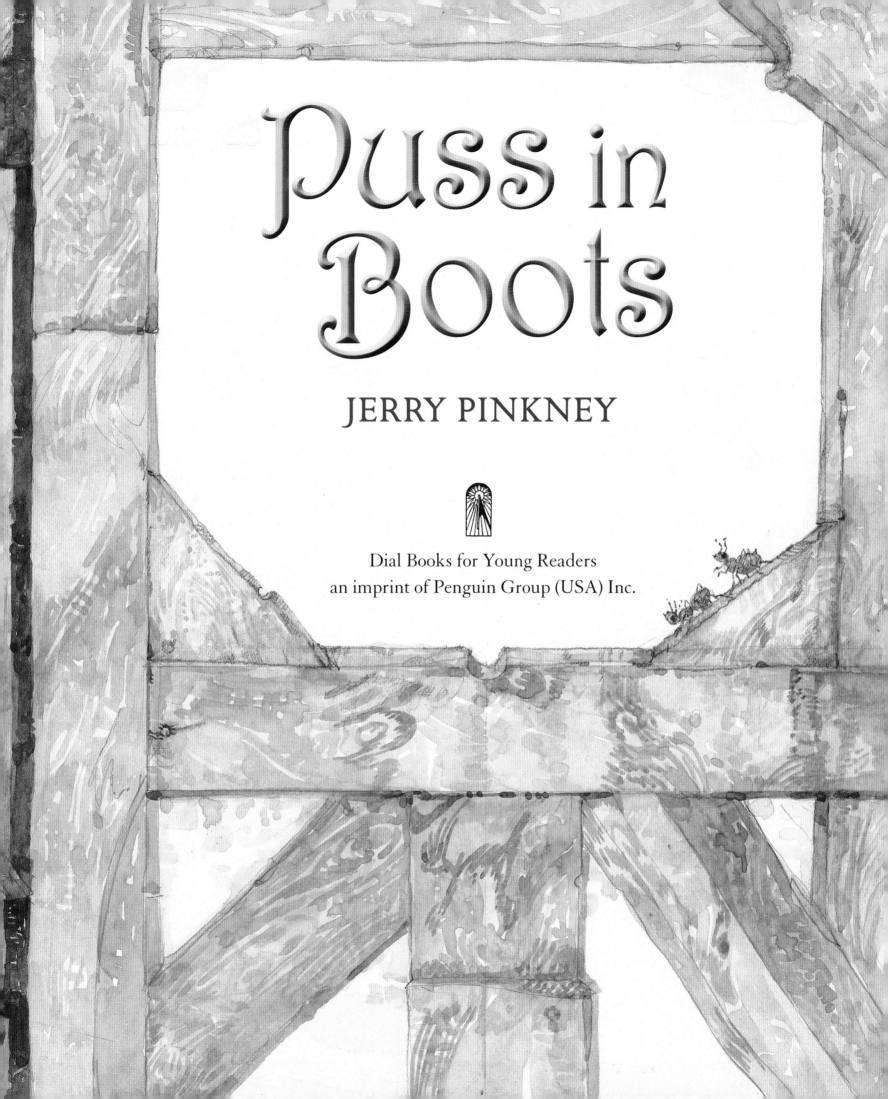

Puss in Boots

JERRY PINKNEY

Dial Books for Young Readers
an imprint of Penguin Group (USA) Inc.

Nestled in the hills of a quaint village sat a grain mill. The miller had three hardworking sons, a donkey, and a cat. When the miller died, his belongings were divided in this order: The oldest son received the mill; the middle son, the donkey; and the youngest, named Benjamin, got the cat.

This worried Benjamin enormously. "Just how can I make my way in this life," he sighed, "with only a cat!"

The cat overheard. "Have some boots made for me," he said, "and give me a strong sack with a drawstring. I just might be able to help you find your fortune." Benjamin knew his cat to be clever, and so he agreed. How gallant the cat looked in his boots, standing upright on hind legs. From that day on, Benjamin called him Puss in Boots.

Puss went about filling the sack with cabbage leaves and carrots, then hauled it into the deep woods, where he knew there was an abundance of rabbits. He laid down a trail of bite-size bits, stretched out as though he were dead, and waited. Before long they came, one hop at a time. One foolish rabbit took the bait, and jumped right into the sack.

Instantly Puss pulled the strings, knotted them, and headed for the king's castle. He knew that a fresh rabbit was just the right present to offer the king, and a way of introduction. Once inside the royal chambers, Puss bowed and placed the rabbit at the king's feet. "I have brought Your Majesty a gift from my young master, the Count of Carabas, with his compliments."

"Tell your count I gladly accept," the king responded. "It will make for a delicious meal."

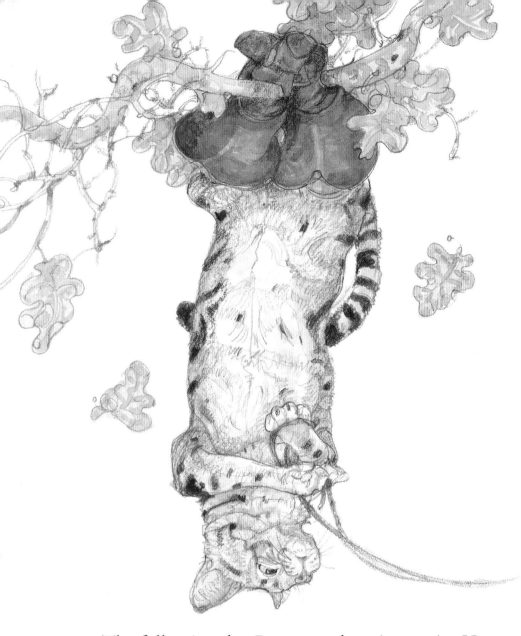

The following day Puss went hunting again. He knew where the partridge fed. This time he hung by his ankles in a tree, with the sack's drawstrings in his paws and kernels of corn as bait. Again, with great patience he waited. When before long he had caught a partridge, Puss returned to the castle, to the delight of the king. Puss continued to surprise the king with gifts—one day a rabbit, the next day a partridge, one day a fish, the next day a pheasant. So it went until the king sent gold in gratitude to the Count of Carabas and had a special feathered hat made for Puss.

One day, as he was leaving, Puss saw the king's men preparing to take His Majesty and the princess for a carriage outing. Right then Puss hatched a plan.

Rushing home, he said to Benjamin, "If you do as I suggest, more fortune will come to you. First, go wash off the dust of the day in the river. Leave the rest to me."

Benjamin did just as Puss asked. After all, had his cat not supplied enough gold for him to provide for himself and even help his brothers?

While Benjamin was bathing, Puss proceeded to hide his master's clothing in a hollow tree. No sooner were they hidden than the king's carriage approached.

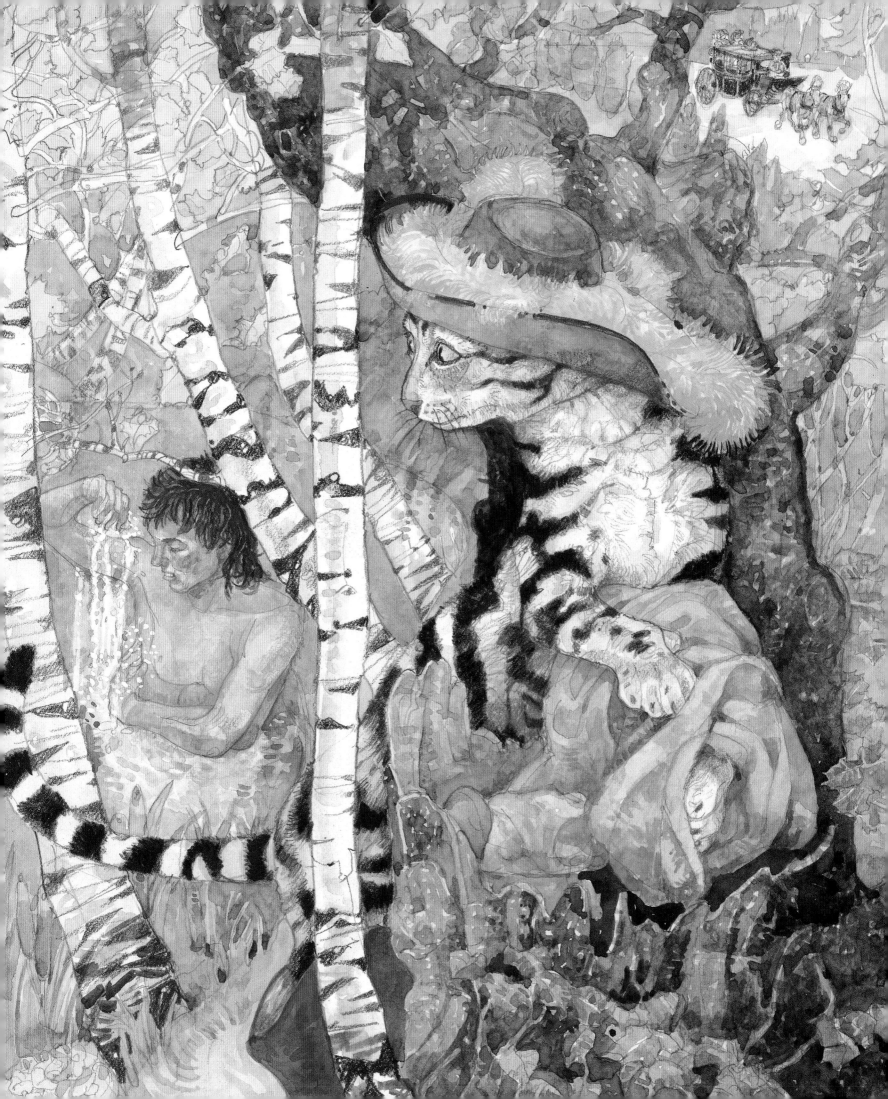

"Help, help!" the cat cried out.

"My lord went for a swim," Puss told the king and his coachman, "and thieves came and stole his clothes. Now the count is in the water and can't get out. If he stays in much longer he will freeze!"

Immediately the king commanded his coachman to rescue the count. Benjamin didn't know what his cat was up to, but he played along. The king's young daughter sent a footman back to the palace to fetch clothing fit for a lord, and soon Benjamin was out of the river and outfitted in fine garments. He felt grand, especially when he was invited to join the king and princess for the rest of their outing. And this pleased Princess Daniella very much, for now she would have someone her age to talk with.

In the meantime the cat, pleased that his plans were succeeding, went ahead of them until he came to a dense forest. He knew these lands belonged to a rich and evil sorcerer. When he met up with countrymen who were clearing away tall trees, he spoke to them in the name of this sorcerer. "The king's carriage will be passing by soon," said he. "If you do not tell the king that this forest belongs to the Count of Carabas, you shall be ground up and made into sausage!" The woodsmen bowed their heads and, trembling, they all agreed.

Soon the carriage passed by, and the king called out to the woodsmen, "To whom does this vast forest belong?"

"The Count of Carabas," they all answered.

Meanwhile Puss, running ahead, met with a group of reapers. "The king's carriage will be passing by soon," said he in the name of the sorcerer. "If you do not tell the king that these fields of wheat belong to the Count of Carabas, you shall be ground up and made into sausage!" Then off he ran.

Moments later the carriage passed by. "Who owns all this land and its golden crop?" called the king. With shaky voices the reapers all shouted, "The Count of Carabas."

Puss soon came to the large estate where the sorcerer dwelled. After passing over a drawbridge he entered the castle's courtyard with its lush grounds. There he spotted many industrious gardeners. "The king's carriage will be arriving here soon," said he in the name of the sorcerer. "If you do not tell the king that these flowers bloom for the Count of Carabas, you shall be ground up and made into sausage!"

Puss was terrified, but after gathering his wits, he said, "A bear is so much like you, great sorcerer. The bear is strong and fearless. How about something graceful and lean. Can you turn yourself into a deer?"

Then Puss marched up the stairs right into the sorcerer's chambers. Bowing, the cunning cat said, "I've heard you have great powers."

The sorcerer sneered. "Beyond all that you can imagine," he crowed, with a laugh that rattled everything on his table.

"Convince me," Puss responded.

"I can turn myself into any animal I choose," boasted the sorcerer. And with that, he let out a ferocious growl, leaped into the air, and became a great bear.

"That's easy," snorted the sorcerer. Oh, how high that deer sprang before the sorcerer turned back into himself.

"Amazing!" Puss exclaimed. "But do you have the power to change yourself into the smallest and weakest of creatures, like, say, a mouse?"

The flattery had made the sorcerer quite silly. "Dear cat," he said, "just watch." Instantly a squeak was heard. Before the sorcerer could scurry out of the room on his tiny mouse paws . . .

Puss had gobbled him right up.

Just about that time the king's carriage crossed the drawbridge and entered the magnificent castle garden. "My countrymen," the king called out, "to whom does this enchanting place belong?"

"The Count of Carabas," they told him, tossing bouquets.

As the carriage arrived at the staircase up to the grandest of castles, even larger and more magnificent than the king's own palace, Count Carabas climbed out to escort the princess and king inside.

When Puss saw them he knew that his work was done. "Your Majesty," the cat announced, "you have arrived at the castle of my master, Count Carabas."

Puss led them into the great hall, which glittered with gold and precious jewels. That day the king decreed that the princess would become the Countess of Carabas. Soon bells were ringing throughout the entire countryside, announcing the royal wedding.

The very next day His Majesty the king bestowed on Puss in Boots the royal title of prime minister. Puss never chased mice again. (That is, never except for his own amusement.)

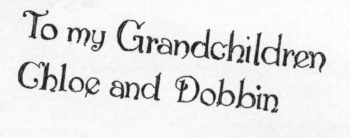

To my Grandchildren Chloe and Dobbin

DIAL BOOKS FOR YOUNG READERS

A division of Penguin Young Readers Group • Published by The Penguin Group • Penguin Group (USA) Inc., 375 Hudson Street, New York, NY 10014, U.S.A. • Penguin Group (Canada), 90 Eglinton Avenue East, Suite 700, Toronto, Ontario, Canada M4P 2Y3 (a division of Pearson Penguin Canada Inc.) • Penguin Books Ltd, 80 Strand, London WC2R 0RL, England • Penguin Ireland, 25 St. Stephen's Green, Dublin 2, Ireland (a division of Penguin Books Ltd) • Penguin Group (Australia), 250 Camberwell Road, Camberwell, Victoria 3124, Australia (a division of Pearson Australia Group Pty Ltd) • Penguin Books India Pvt Ltd, 11 Community Centre, Panchsheel Park, New Delhi - 110 017, India • Penguin Group (NZ), 67 Apollo Drive, Rosedale, Auckland 0632, New Zealand (a division of Pearson New Zealand Ltd) • Penguin Books (South Africa) (Pty) Ltd, 24 Sturdee Avenue, Rosebank, Johannesburg 2196, South Africa • Penguin Books Ltd, Registered Offices: 80 Strand, London WC 2R 0RL, England

The publisher does not have any control over and does not assume any responsibility for author or third-party websites or their content. Designed by Lily Malcom • Text set in Granjon • Manufactured in China on acid-free paper • 10 9 8 7 6 5 4 3 2 1

Library of Congress Cataloging-in-Publication Data • Pinkney, Jerry. • Puss in Boots / Jerry Pinkney. • p. cm. • Summary: A clever cat wins for his master a fortune and the hand of a princess. • ISBN 978-0-8037-1642-1 (hardcover) • [1. Fairy tales. 2. Folklore—France.] I. Title. • PZ8.P575Pu 2012 • 398.2—dc23 • [E] 2011038789

The full-color artwork was prepared using graphite, color pencil, and watercolor.

A Note from the Artist

I had been ruminating on adapting Puss in Boots for some time, deeply fascinated with this classic fairy tale. The idea of a talking cat, dressed in dapper boots and standing upright, excited and tested my visual sensibilities.

Puss in Boots by Charles Perrault was first published in France in 1697, then translated and published in England in 1729. I staged my reimagining in France at the time of the story's English edition. I used Cole's *Best-Loved Folktales of the World* and Lang's *The Blue Fairy Book* with its black-and-white illustrations as a source for early versions. It very well could have been those early drawings that led me to make Puss a black-and-white silver-tabby British shorthair.

I then went about borrowing as many illustrated versions of Puss in Boots as my local library could locate. The exact tally I did not keep, but I'm positive the books numbered more than twenty. The reviewing of that wide range of interpretations heightened my desire to adapt the tale through my personal lens. Those books were the beginning of a stream of inspiration that caused me to be more inventive.

The next step was the search for visual reference on France of that time period, its costuming, mills, castles, horse-drawn coaches, and landscapes. Oh, how I marveled at the flair of over-the-top fashions and gardens, the majestic scale of the buildings.

With all in place, I began my sketching and reworking of the text. The process went back and forth between the two, with each step molding my vision for this time-honored tale. I expanded the story to have the king give Puss a feathered hat in appreciation of the cat's gifts, thus strengthening their relationship. My favorite section, at first daunting and thus a fuel for my creative juices, was the ogre's transformation, from bear to deer to mouse. I chose creatures native to France, and included a fold-out for a cinematic feel.

In deciding to end the story with Puss receiving the honorable title of Ambassador, I have given him the status that he alone deserved; and I've hinted, on the back endpapers, at future adventures that I hope will inspire my readers' own big imaginations.